BLUE MURDER

David E Burke

Also by the Author

The Fiesta Murders
Book two in the Menorca Detective Series

To my wife for her patient help and my family for all their support. To Agatha, Douglas and Ian and, most of all, Menorca for their inspiration.

CONTENTS

1

THE RED TIDE

The entire sea, as far as could be seen from the shoreline of
Binibeca beach, was a sickly pink. It would be quite a
shock for anyone arriving this day and expecting to find the
usual crystal clear turquoise water that is the hallmark of
Menorca's surrounding seas.

The reason? Every few years since the late 1990's an
explosion in the Jellyfish population has occurred in the
Med during the winter months. This has been attributed to
various factors – global warming, an increase in the
available food supply, a lack of predators...

Whatever the cause, the Balearics and some mainland
Spanish resorts see an invasion of Jellyfish each year, with
creatures ranging in diameter from a few inches to the size
of a dustbin lid. Menorca, being an island slap bang in the
middle of the western Med, is one of the first unfortunate
places to encounter this unpleasant influx.

The locals call this phenomenon *'La Marea Roja'* or 'The Red Tide'

It is due to the fact that *Medusas* - the millions of nasties making up the main mass of this glutinous floating carpet - are pinkish-red in colour.

The effect, as the tides funnel these unwelcome visitors into Menorca's small inlets and calas, is of the sea turning from a pleasing Turquoise to a sickly Fuchsia.

Of course, the one thing everyone knows about Jellyfish is that they sting. The toxins released by their needle-like tendrils can be extremely painful and leave burn-like scars that can last for years.

Experienced swimmers and divers know all too well to watch out for the telltale floating domes and hanging tendrils. The slightest touch can feel like a cigarette being stubbed out on your skin. Once stung, never forgotten.

Enough stings from enough *Medusas* could even kill an adult human. So it would be very unlikely that anyone would be foolhardy enough to enter the water upon seeing a Red Tide.

So why on this March morning in this gentle horseshoe shaped bay was there a man in the water?

Floating face down. Fully clothed.

Clearly dead.

2

ANOTHER DAY IN PARADISE

Frank Harmer sat on his patio, sipped his breakfast coffee and watched yet another spur-thighed tortoise make its ponderous way along the edge of his swimming pool.

It was one of the many rare species of fauna that seemed to thrive in Menorca's unspoilt natural environment which was, unsurprisingly, a UNESCO designated biosphere reserve.

What primeval force motivated them to follow the same steadfast path each Menorcan spring he could only guess at. Probably the urge to procreate. Somewhere, perhaps at a neighbouring garden was another randy spur-thighed tortoise heading in this one's direction. And maybe they would eventually meet up and fall passionately into a shell like embrace and make slow turtle love.

Frank chuckled at the thought, and took another sip of coffee. He sat back, and sighed contentedly as the warm breeze stirred the leaves on the lemon trees that lined his garden wall and wafted the delicious scent to him. Yes, another sunny, tortoise-paced day in paradise.

He mused at how different his life was compared to a year ago. The muggy morning commute in a packed train carriage. The sterile dimly lit offices of the Met. The daily stream of meetings and briefings, phone calls and emails. The endless paperwork and report filling. The hurried lunches in a noisy canteen or crowded coffee bar. The late journey home. A take-away or microwaved meal, followed by several large scotches.

And finally, to bed. Or falling asleep on the couch to the blabber of a late night movie.

He shuddered at the memory, then yawned, and stretched out in the capacious wicker armchair.

Yes, this was the life! Here in a pretty Villa in the heart of Menorca's favourite ex-pat haven - the well-manicured and peaceful village of Trebaluger.

This had been a second home for more than 7 years. He and Linda had bought it after they'd fallen in love with the island and vowed to retire here. Now that time had come, though sadly without Linda. When offered early retirement and a handsome golden handshake from the Met, the opportunity had proven irresistible.

Now he, Francis Michael Harmer was living the dream. And yet something was missing. Something he couldn't quite put his finger on. Paradise wasn't perfect without Linda he knew, but still, there was something else missing.

'Francis'. He'd always disliked that name. He always thought it sounded fey.

Now 'Frank, on the other hand… that was a solid name. A name you could trust. Good old Frank.

Detective Inspector Frank Harmer. It should have been Superintendent Frank Harmer in his and his wife's opinion, had he not been constantly passed over for promotion when the opportunity came. The assessment boards always found some reason, some excuse. His superiors were consistently praising his performance, yet when the final decision came, it was always in favour of one of the other candidates.

It became an embarrassment to him as he approached his mid-fifties. Despite a glowing career with a phenomenal arrest and conviction record, he still remained a Detective Inspector. He suspected new technology was to blame. Not that he was a Luddite. He had embraced computers in the workplace, albeit with less enthusiasm than many of his colleagues.

However, he felt it was a certain 'incident' that was his undoing, rather than his digital reticence. It happened in the 80's when the Met had first introduced desktop computers networked into the police mainframe.

At first, just the secretaries were using them. Then the junior officers, clerks and caseworkers.

Then finally the managers and senior officers – many of whom had never touched a typewriter keyboard and had been used to delegating such tasks - were required to attend training courses and enter the brave new world of the microprocessor.

It took Frank a long time to get used to his Apple SEII. He approached it each morning like a man wary of a sleeping viper. He often forgot his password or a keystroke command or simply could not locate the whereabouts of an important file that he urgently needed.

One particularly frustrating morning, when he was desperate to print out a case document for a court attendance for which he was running late, it wasn't so much a 'booting up' issue as a 'booting out' ... through his open 3rd floor office window.

The machine fell like a large and expensive paperweight – much as Frank regarded it - 30 feet onto the hard tarmac of the car park below and shattered into a thousand pieces.

It narrowly missed the Chief's prized classic Jaguar, and had it been 30 seconds earlier might have landed on the Chief himself. He had just entered the building and came running back out to see what the hell was going on.

A strong reprimand and a small leave of absence later it was all over the Met.

It earned him the nickname of 'The Terminator', a highly popular film at the time. Henceforth, he was branded a technophobe. Eventually he became an avid PC user when he was made deskbound, thanks to the bullet that shattered his right knee during a hostage siege at an East End Seafood Restaurant.

He had almost talked the man into surrendering when some nervous young cop discharged his weapon, shattering the glass of a large fish tank and causing the hostage-taker to fire his own gun, which he was lowering but was unfortunately still pointing at Frank at the time.

After several reconstructive surgeries and many months of therapy before he could walk again. Getting out of bed was often difficult and painful.

Some days he took a lot of painkillers; some days he needed a walking stick. So, gone were the days of chasing a fleeing criminal down an alleyway or across the back gardens of a housing estate and then rugby tackling him to the ground.

From then on he swore by his iMac. It was the Internet that made the difference. He found it to be an indispensable communication and information-gathering tool.

And still, though he remained one of the best detectives on the force, with a reputation for tracking down villains and

solving difficult cases, others, perhaps less capable but more adept at sucking up to their superiors, continued to be promoted over his head.

So when the chance of early retirement came along with a handsome lump sum and very nice pension, it was an offer he couldn't refuse.

And now here he was, living the good life in sunny Menorca.

His mind wandered back to the early days. When he and Linda had first discovered the island. They'd originally planned a trip to Mallorca, the island's larger sister and most famous of the Balearic chain.

But due to a protracted court case where Frank was witness for the state, they'd had to reschedule and book a last minute break.

Being July and the peak holiday period, decent hotels were thin on the ground. But the travel agent recommended the La Quinta - a 5 Star at Cala'n Bosch in the south west of Menorca. It was expensive but it looked amazing, and besides, they really needed a break.

They fell in love with the island and went back every summer, trying a different resort each time. Eventually, they knew they wanted to retire here and started looking for their dream home.

After several house hunting trips in the low seasons, they found it at Trebalugar, an idyllic Menorcan village sat at the South Eastern edge of the island, just a few kilometres from the Capital City of Mahon.

Frank remembered their first sight of the villa on that slightly misty and muggy March morning, and began reminiscing about those first exciting and happy months setting up home here in this Villa. It had been built in the early 1980's and more recently refurbished.

He and Linda had fallen completely in love with its old Hacienda style, its rotunda lounge, its covered patio adorned with grapevine, its arched doorways, and well-stocked gardens - the riot of Bougainvillea that overran the exterior.

Then there was that quirky little Menorcan gate that squeaked every time you...

The phone rang and made him jump. He got up and answered.

The caller spoke good English with a strong Spanish accent. 'Señor Harmer?'

'Yes. Who's this?'

'This is Juan Diego Rodriguez. Inspector de Policia in Mahon. We met at the Acalde's - the Mayor's Gala Evening in January.'

'Yes. I remember. How are you Juan?'

'Oh alls or nothings. You know how it goes.'

'Yes, I do.'

Frank could picture him now. A thickset middle-aged man with salt and pepper beard, and an engaging personality. Frank had warmed to him right away. He seemed to know a lot about Frank and his career, regaling him for most of the evening with some of Frank's most famous cases.

He quoted them at length and in the sort of detail that would usually be associated with an obsessive celebrity fan. More detail than Frank himself could remember. He was flattered and impressed by the man's knowledge of his exploits.

Juan cleared his throat nervously, as if he had something awkward to ask.

'I know you are retired Señor Harmer.'

'Call me Frank please.'

'Of course. It is a bit of a, as you say it, an imposition, but I wonder if I could ask for your assistance? That is if you are interested in this case.'

'This case'. Frank felt an old familiar spark begin to kindle in his stomach.

'Er…well I…'

'It would be in an advisory capacity, of course!'

'Of course…tell me more. What's it about?'

There was a lengthy pause as Juan Diego decided how much to impart on the phone.

'There's a body in the bay of Binibeca. And there is something… most strange. I'd like your opinion, if you would be so kind as to join me at the crime scene.'

Frank was intrigued but knew not to ask for any more detail on the phone. He felt the spark in his gut turn into an old and familiar flame.

Yes. That was it. That's what was missing in Paradise. A purpose. A crime to solve. A case.

'I'll be there in half an hour.'

3

'SEE THE MAN IN EVENING CLOTHES...'

The drive to Binibeca was uneventful and short. Compared to the UK, nothing was very far away on an island just 22 by 10 miles. It was equivalent to living on the Isle of Wight, but with more sunshine and better beaches.

He always enjoyed this short trip down to the little Cala through the quaint and typically Menorcan town of Sant Luis with its orange tree lined streets and the brightly coloured shop and café awnings. Then the winding drive through small hamlets and goat farms. And finally down gentle slopes to the prosaic little fishing village of Binibeca.

But this day he barely noticed a thing. His mind was occupied. It had been so long since he had been involved in a case that he could barely contain his excitement. Perhaps it was a just an unfortunate bather. But in March? Unlikely. Tourists hadn't yet arrived and you'd be lucky to see any locals in the water before May.

Perhaps a diver or sailing enthusiast? The recent storms and high tides would tend to rule that out. Ah! A surfer! Rough seas would bring them out. Nothing like the prospect of 30 foot waves to get them into their steamers and waxing their boards!

Yet Juan Diego had said there was something very odd about it.

The ornate white stucco buildings of Binibeca Vell rose up to meet him as the little Opel Agila sped down the approach road that led to the quaint coastal resort. It looked like its picture postcard and always reminded Frank of a large Christmas cake. As if all the villas and houses were covered with white icing sugar. The strict *Ayuntamiento* rules here insisted that every building complied with a strict colour code – white, white or white.

It was one of the prettiest little old fishing villages you could find in the Balearics. Only it wasn't that old. It was merely purpose-built to look that way. In the 1960's the island elders decided that one thing that Menorca lacked was its own authentic old fishing village. So they created one – Binibeca Vell. It brought the tourists flocking in.

However, Binibeca Nou, the newer residential side where Frank was heading now, set above the resort's small but perfectly formed horseshoe bay, was a different affair.

Unlike it's faux other half, it was festooned with a mishmash of modern villas of every size, and style from bijou to super luxury.

Frank drove to the lower beach car park, which was now cordoned off with police tape. He was waved to a nearby empty roadside space by an armed Guardia Civil Officer. He parked and took the narrow winding path that led down from the car park through a small wooded copse to the beach.

The air was thick with the smell of pine, wild rosemary and gorse, and he enjoyed the aromatic mix as he made his way through the trees.

Many rich scented and colourful shrubs grew in this gentle temperate climate. It was one of the things he really loved about Menorca. He delighted in the Hibiscus and Oleander that bordered many gardens, and the Clematis and Wisteria that adorned the villa walls.

He walked across the beach to where Juan Diego and his forensic team stood around the body lying at the water's edge. The soft yielding sand crept into his shoes and the uneven balance caused a familiar twinge of pain in his right knee and hip. He cursed the fact that in his eagerness he had left his walking stick at home. He often found he rarely used it here. Unlike the UK the warm Menorcan climate seemed to have miraculous pain-relieving properties.

Not today.

The forensic photographer was walking around the body clicking away under the guidance of Inspector Juan who looked up as Frank arrived. He smiled broadly and thrust out his hand.

'Señor Harmer. How good of you to come.'

Frank shook his hand 'Call me Frank, please.'

Frank was glad that Juan did not attempt the customary Menorcan greeting of a kiss on each cheek. He could never work out the etiquette of it. Which occasion called for it? When was it socially acceptable with the same sex?

No, a handshake was just fine.

Juan then turned to one side and looked down at the body. Though there was a thin blanket placed over the head, it was clear that this was a man, fully clothed, average height and slightly built.

"See the man in evening clothes, how he got here I don't know." The voice of Rod Stewart rang through Frank's mind. An appropriate song always did on these occasions.

Juan told the photographer to suspend his activities momentarily.

Although it was obvious Frank said 'Evening clothes!'

Juan nodded. 'Yes, he was…how do you put it? Dressed up for the nines?'

The deceased was wearing a formal black dinner jacket and dress trousers.

'Yes' Agreed Frank 'Except for the shoes!'

The man wasn't wearing any. Or socks.

He added. 'No watch, or rings. Nothing to identify him? Did you recognise the face?'

Juan looked grim and called to an officer who carefully lifted the thin sheet covering the man's head. Frank felt the breath leave his body. Closely followed by the urge to vomit.

The man's face was so badly swollen by Jellyfish stings that it wasn't so much a face, but a purple and red balloon that someone had tried to draw a face on in the dark.

Years of hardened experience kicked-in and the urge to vomit subsided.

'Huh! His own Mother would not recognise him. I think every *Medusa* in the bay has stung him. More than once *eh amigo*?'

He laughed and then noted the serious expression on Frank's face.

'But I think he is someone important yes? The suit. It is *de lujo*.'

He pulled at the collar with the stick of driftwood to reveal a very exclusive clothing label.

Frank said 'Well, that should narrow it down… if he's a local.'

Juan nodded. 'Si. There can't be many peoples with that kind of money here.'

This was true. Although Menorca had attracted many wealthy Brit retirees to its shores, most were living comfortably on their ex-pat pensions. The really rich went to the more cosmopolitan and culturally hip climes of Ibiza and Mallorca. Still there were a few wealthy ex-pats and native Menorcans. The odd mansion and family estate still adorned the odd hilltop.

Frank's brow furrowed, deep in thought. 'Of course, he could have just slipped and fallen off a boat?'

Juan shook his head and pulled a doubting face. 'A gin palace? At his time of the year? With these waves and swells? I doubt it.'

Gin Palaces. That was the derisory term the locals used for the fancy luxury yachts that adorned the more showy harbour fronts at Mahon and Ciutadella, usually in the high summer months when the island was thronging with tourists. They sported nameplates such as 'Lotto Dosh' and Done Banking'.

In July and August, they were dutifully trotted out like trophy wives and parked at the private jetties in front of the posh eateries that ran the length of Menorca's two main cities' harbours. The rest of the year they remained sealed in airtight plastic wraps in large sheds on Menorcan industrial estates or *Polígonos*.

The two men strolled back up the beach as the police photographer and forensic team finished up their work. Both were momentarily lost in thought. The sunlight glinting off the side of a small jeep turning in the road above the beach caught Frank's eye and broke his train of thought.

He stopped suddenly and said. 'I think the man, whoever he was, was killed. But it was not an accident.'

Juan, lighting yet another cigarette, stared at him and then smiled slowly.

This was why he'd invited Frank along. He felt excitement at the prospect of Frank making one of his legendary analyses.

'Really? What makes you say this is not an accident?' Juan continued lighting the cigarette feigning nonchalance.

Frank shut his eyes and examined the evidence. Having an eye for small details was a big asset for a detective. It had served him well during his career and it felt good to see if the old cogs would still turn.

'Well, let's see… you found no wallet or any other form of ID…his watch and wedding ring are missing, the tan lines tell us that much. Yes, those items could have come off in the water, but it's unlikely. Not all of them.

No, it looks like someone doesn't want him identified. Grey hair, and judging by the liver spots on the un-stung skin of his hands, which by the way tells us he was dead before the Jellies got to him as he clearly didn't try to shield his face, I would put him in his late sixties or early seventies. His tie is missing, could have taken it off, but my guess is it was removed.'

He looked to see if Juan was following this. Juan was enraptured. Now Frank had the bit between his teeth.

He went on. 'Probably an expat. Did you see how white the skin was where his watch had been? Heavy smoker judging by the nicotine stain on his right thumb and index finger, which also tells us he was right-handed.'

Frank could see Juan was impressed. The policeman was mesmerised. He nodded mechanically for Frank to continue.

'His face is too messed up for it just to have been the work of *Medusas*. I'd say he was beaten with something. A metal bar or a baseball bat.'

Frank was getting into his stride. 'His jaw looks broken. His left arm too. Then there's the shoes, or lack of them. Not sure where that fits in…yet. But I would say there is enough evidence to say this man is the victim of a violent assault.'

Juan looked stunned. He dropped the half-finished cigarette into the sand and clapped his hands. 'Bravo Señor Harmer! Bravo!'

Frank blushed. He hadn't meant to show off. It just felt so good to be doing what he loved doing most. Solving crimes.

'Well, it's all conjecture at this point…'

'No, no!' Juan insisted. He was seriously impressed and felt honoured to see his hero in action and living up to, and even beyond his expectations. 'I trust your guts.'

An ambulance made its way past them down the small track to the beach. They watched it slowly plough through the sand toward the waiting officers and body bag.

Frank said 'Well, I'm sure you and your boys will be able to sort it all out with no further help from me.'

Juan looked horrified. 'No, please. Your insights are invaluable. I spoke to the chief just this morning and he said we are to… ah yes, to extend you every courtesy. It will be an honour for us to be working with such a great English detective.

He laughed and then added. 'Perhaps some of your guts will rub off onto us too. No?'

They walked back through trees to the car park. A battered looking Rav 4 Jeep was just pulling out from the kerb, the two male occupants staring at them as it went by, perhaps curious at the goings on and at not being able to access the beach which was cordoned off with police crime scene tape.

Frank shook Juan's hand once more. 'Well if I can be of more help…'

'Yes, yes. Please keep thinking and call me if anything else comes to your mind. Meanwhile we will do our forensics examinations. Try to identify this unfortunate person.'

'Well if I were you I'd start by checking the clubs. Sailing, Rotary, Cricket Club. That sort of thing. Remember we're looking for a retired, pipe or cigar smoking, expat with a bob or two.'

Juan looked a little confused 'Bob? Who is…'

'Sorry, it's an old English expression. It means he was wealthy.'

Frank had an idea. He asked 'Who do we know that knows everyone who is anyone on this island?'

Juan smiled and they both said the answer out loud.

'Charlie Mack!'

4

TEA FOR TWO

Charles Mackay (aka Charlie Mack) knew everyone who was anyone in Menorca. Founder of the island's most successful Villa Management Company, he enjoyed unrivalled status and respect among both the Spanish and expat British business communities.

A stocky and amiable Scotsman with a shock of red hair and a broad brogue of an accent, he was president of the Menorca Rotary Club and honorary member of the local Chamber of Commerce, leading charity benefactor, guest speaker, event opener, and beloved employer to a significant number of people in his island chain of offices.

Having dual citizenship in Spain and the UK, thanks to having a Spanish Mum hailing from Barcelona and a born and bred Glaswegian for a Father, he had the considerable advantage of being able to speak Spanish, Catalan and English like a native.

His natural charm and gentle humour, made him a great salesman. He'd learned a lot from his father, a sales manager for a popular brand of Whisky.

Since the very opening of his business '*Villas Perfectas*' right at the start of the 80's property boom, Charlie had made a point of getting to personally know every British and Menorcan businessperson, government official, politician and social bigwig on the island.

He called them all by their first names. He asked after the health of their families, he never missed a birthday and always sent presents. He helped significantly with local charities, got new schools built, supported amateur and professional sports clubs, and often helped start-up businesses get off the ground with private loans and by using his many influential contacts.

At the age of 67, he was a well-known figure around the Mahon port as he daily swung his blue Daimler up from the harbour road and into his very own private parking space at the top of the hill opposite the famous fish and meat markets and under the shadow of the *Iglesia de Santa María* spire that towered over this very congested area. He was one of the only individuals in Menorca ever to have this privilege.

It was the rarest of concessions but granted with special dispensation by the *Ayuntamiento de Mahón* for this special man.

His PA tapped lightly at his office door and ushered Frank into the room. A massive beam of a smile crossed Charlie's face. He stood up and warmly pumped Frank's hand.

'Frank. Good to see you again. How's Trebaluger?' Then noticing Frank's slight limp, 'That wee leg still giving you gyp?'

'Oh. Can't complain.' Both men sat down. Frank, in the well-upholstered guest chair and Charlie back behind his capacious antique desk.

'Coffee? Tea? A dram?'

'Coffee thanks.'

'Right. Never touch it me. Coffee not the Scotch. Bit of a teapot. Have it flown in. Menorcans know how to make great coffee, and Gin, but they've not got a clue when it comes to a good brew.'

'Well in that case, I'll join you in a tea. I've not had a decent cuppa myself for a while.'

Charlie buzzed the desk intercom and his secretary came back in.

'Tea for two Catalina hen.' He smiled at her.

'Milk and sugar?" she enquired of Frank.

'Milk and one please. *Gracias*.'

'*De nada*,' the pretty dark haired young girl smiled back and went to make the tea in the method that Charlie had shown her. "You've got to heat the pot, y'see! Proper tea leaves too, not them wee bags on strings!'

By now Catalina had got it down to a fine art and always felt a warm glow of pride when Charlie took his first sip and said, "Ahhhh, lovely. Aye a proper cuppa is that!"

Charlie sat back and said 'Right Laddie, let's talk about this terrible thing that's happened here. Evenin clothes y'say? No shoes? Hmmm.'

He sat back and thought about all that Frank had told him of the man in the bay.

'Well it sounds like a boating accident. Someone from a posh yacht y'ken. Except…'

Frank gave him an enquiring look.

'Well, not much pleasure cruising done this time of the year, not with the sea conditions and the recent storms?'

'Easy to check though. I'll call the *Maritimo*'s Office and see if anyone's been daft enough to brave the wild briney.'

'If someone's gone missing, then we'll soon be hearing about it nay doubt. Someone's friend or partner's going to be looking for them. I expect the Chief of Police is getting a call right now. So the mystery man will soon have a name, if not a face!'

He chuckled and added 'Hope it's not someone that owes me money. Or anyone from my poker group. That's ma second source of income!'

Frank laughed with him. Charlie always did know how to put a light-hearted spin on a dark subject matter. His humour was infectious.

'Right. Enough of this nasty business. Why not pop around to my place this weekend if you're not doing anything. Having a bit of a do. Nothing formal just friends and some posh nosh to christen my new Tennis Court. Bring your kit and we'll have a round robin if it's no too cold eh?'

Tennis was Charlie's big passion and everyone knew it. He sometimes came into the office in his tennis gear, coming straight from the Tennis Club on the outskirts of the capital.

It was not Frank's idea of fun, but he thanked Charlie for the kind invitation and said he would try to make it. He wouldn't. He did not like the idea of spending a long afternoon listening to well-heeled expat retirees talking about their boats, portfolios and gardens ad-nauseum.

They chatted a while longer about the local restaurants and the weather, and Charlie enquired as to how Frank was settling in to life on the island. Frank gave him an update and then announced he would have to leave to pick up some fish for his evening meal.

The fish market stalls were often sold out of the best stuff by late morning, after the locals and restauranteurs had come and had their pick of the catch.

Charlie accompanied Frank to the reception area of the building, as he did with all of his guests. 'Okay, I'll make some calls and if I hear anything I'll let you know right away.'

Frank thanked him and headed off to the fish market.
It was a beautiful old market building set at the top of the hill and winding road that ran down to the harbour.

The clamour of buyers and stallholders and stench of fish was quite heady. But it was always a joyful atmosphere to be in, as long as you weren't too squeamish.

While studying the colourful myriad of freshly caught fishes, many of them still moving, the thought occurred to him that there may be some clues or evidence lurking on the sea bed near the mouth of Binibeca Bay. After all, there were several items of clothing and possessions missing from the body.

They could have easily come off in the water and be lying on the sea bed. The water wasn't too deep there, 5 or 6 meters at the most. Yes, it would be worth a dive to take a look-see. Besides, he loved diving and hadn't been out since last Autumn.

On returning to his car with a bag of fresh *Langostinos*, he called Ignacio, the proprietor of and head diver at Menorca Sur Sub Aqua.

He asked him to get things ready for a dive the next morning. *Medusas* willing of course! Ignacio said it would depend on the sea conditions but that the forecast was good, so a dive was possible. Best to get it done soon, he told himself, before the next storm had a chance to wash away or cover up anything.

There might be nothing to find. Or there could be a clue waiting that would answer the questions of who was this man? Why was he killed?

More importantly, who was his killer?

5

MARISOL

He parked the Agila in the street, just down from his house, in the space allotted for residents.

This meant, as usual, he had no choice but to walk past the entrance of his neighbour's house. Its drive fronted by the traditional rustic style Menorcan Gate that adorned most rural homes on the island.

As he drew near the front door opened. He hurried on and out of the corner of his eye saw a familiar figure.

'Señor Harmer?' It was his neighbour, Marisol Sanchez.

She lived on her own with her two Siamese cats. They often came over the adjoining garden wall to sleep under his Oliander bushes on hotter days. An attractive middle-aged widow, a records clerk for the *Ayuntamiento de Mahón*,

She had moved to Menorca from Madrid several years ago, where she had lived with her husband until his unfortunate and sudden passing. It had been a happy marriage and they had been blessed with two children, a boy and a girl, both grown up now. She tried to start a new life on the island and put the pain of he loss behind her. But, being a very sociable and lively person, she sometimes she found living alone very difficult.

She was always eager to stop and chat whenever he bumped into her. Which seemed to Frank to be quite often. Unfortunately, he wasn't in the mood right now. He had other things on his mind. But she was so nice, he did not want to offend her.

He turned with feigned surprise and said 'Oh hello. How are you Marisol?' Then added 'Please call me Frank.'

'Of course. I am fine Señor Frank. It's hot today, yes?' She came down the short garden path and stood behind the gate. She was wearing a pink and cream candy-striped blouse and pale green leggings, both closely fitting enough to show that she had a slim but shapely figure.

Frank tried not to stare, but he had to admit she was a very attractive woman. His gaze fell momentarily to her chest and the Shark Tooth pendant that nestled in her cleavage.

Her gaze met his as he looked up and he felt embarrassed.

But she smiled simply and said 'Do you like them? They were a gift from my husband.'

He was taken aback by her frankness. But then, in his experience Spanish people could be very direct.

'Er…yes. They are quite lovely.'

She looked pleased with his response and said 'My husband was quite proud of them.'

'Oh. Was he a plastic surgeon?'

She looked at him quizzically. 'No. He was an accountant, but he loved shark fishing.'

She touched the pendant lightly with her fingers. 'I have to be careful with them. They are quite sharp.'

Realising his mistake Frank decided a change of subject might be in order. 'Isn't it hot for March. They say it is the *El Niño*'

'Quite so. Would you like some Iced Tea? I was just about to have some myself.' She opened the gate.

He hated to be rude. 'Er..well, er… yes. I have a few moments.' He followed along the path into the house and through to the kitchen diner. It was brightly coloured, and throughout the house the rooms were decorated in typical Menorcan style with small paintings of island scenery, wall tiles with hand painted designs, dried flowers in ornate clay vases and polished stone floor tiles.

She gestured for him to sit at the small table, where he noticed two tumblers already placed there.

She produced a large glass pitcher of iced tea from the fridge and poured.

'You are busy on a big case, yes?'

'Why do you say that?'

'The body. On the beach, at Binibeca. Everyone is talking about this.'

'Word certainly travels fast here!'

She laughed. 'There are no secrets in Menorca.'

'Yes. I'm beginning to see that.' He took a long drink and realised how thirsty he was.

'Do you like Muffin?'

'Pardon?'

'Some Muffin…cake. Are you hungry and would you like some?'

That was the other thing. Every time he met her. Every conversation. She kept saying these suggestive things. He couldn't make up his mind if it was just her limited knowledge of English phrasing or if she was coming on to him.

But then, she did have a great figure, and a very alluring smile…

He suddenly realised that he was in fact very hungry. With so much excitement he hadn't stopped to think about food. Now it was mid-afternoon and his stomach was beginning to rebel.

He should go home and have some lunch. It was the excuse he needed to get away. Yet he did not want to seem rude.

While he was debating how to answer, Marisol returned from the kitchen with a tray of iced muffins. They looked delicious.

'Why not.' He took one and smiled at her. 'Been on the go since breakfast!'

She sat opposite and looked around theatrically. Then she leant forward and in a Sotto Voce voice asked 'So who was this 'body'. Has there been foul playing?'

'Eh? Oh, not sure. Looks like a Brit. A local. Dressed in a DJ!'

'He was a disc jockey?'

'No. No. He was wearing a dinner jacket… dressed in evening clothes, as if he was going out to a gala dinner, or something like that.'

'Oh. That is very odd.'

She thought for a moment, her brow knitted in concentration, then said 'Perhaps he was robbed, killed and then dumped into the water. On his way home from somewhere. A restaurant or a night club.'

Frank continued the thought 'Or he could have been at a dinner party on a big yacht, had a bit too much to drink and he fell off the boat, hit his head on something, rocks maybe, and drowned. The morning tide then brought him into the bay.'

She considered this for a moment. 'Yes. That would make much sense. But I am guessing there is more that makes you think otherways.'

'Yes. It's the shoes. Or rather, the lack of them.'

She smiled and raised her eyebrows. 'No shoes?'

'No watch. No tie. No rings and no socks'

'No socks!' She gave him a very serious look and then burst into laughter.

Frank reddened slightly as he realised she was teasing him. 'You're right.' He stumbled. There's probably a simple explanation for it. But still...

'Something bothers your detective's nose, yes? You smell something fishy at Binibeca, no?'

Frank nodded but couldn't help laughing.

She sighed and leaned forward, resting her elbows on the table and chin on her cupped hands and gazed dreamily into his eyes and said 'Don't you just love it at Binibeca. At sunset. It is so peaceful there.'

Frank nervously coughed out some of his muffin.

She went on 'Lying in the sand…bathing naked in the cool waters.''

'What? Ah yes.' He struggled on. 'It is er…very nice.'
'Perhaps, one day we will both come together there!'

'Good heavens! Is that the time?' He looked at his watch, and standing up said. 'I've got an important er…   phone call to make. Thanks for the tea!'

He hurried to the door and not to wanting to seem ungrateful for her hospitality added. 'I really enjoyed your muffin.'

Marisol sat there shaking her head and smiling. Was Señor Frank interested in her?

After all, he keeps saying these things!

6

INTO THE BLUE AGAIN

The following morning at the Menorca Sur Sub Aqua Centre, two men were waiting for him on the dock - a wide concrete apron that skirted the Centre, complete with slipway.

The taller and thicker-set of the two was Ignacio, owner of Menorca Sur Sub Aqua.

Frank could hear them chatting away in Spanish as he approached.

They were stood just outside the doorway of the centre's small office and shop. An air tank and scuba gear were placed neatly on the ground, ready for a dive. Ignacio was talking loudly with his business partner and fellow diving instructor, José.

They looked up as he approached, and a broad toothy grin split Ignacio's well-tanned face. Both he and José were athletic young men in their early thirties and both strikingly good-looking. He could see why their diving school was very popular with both ladies and men alike. Ignacio extended his hand and shook Frank's vigorously.

'Señor Frank, my friend. How are you today? Good?'

'We have not seen you since the 'fireworks' chimed in José, spreading his hands in the air to simulate rockets exploding and then bent over whilst making a vomiting sound and using his hands to simulate vomit coming from his mouth.

Both men broke into raucous laughter.

Frank felt a little embarrassed and shuddered at the memory.

At the annual Fiesta in the port of Mahón, most of the island's population turned out to watch the fireworks at midnight on the last day, culminating with the famous underwater rockets. Last year 'Señor Frank' had had a tad too much Gin *Pomada* to drink and just at the moment when the fireworks were about to begin, and all the harbour lights were extinguished, and a hush descended on the expectant crowd massed above the harbour - he had thrown up copiously and noisily, causing much laughter and comment from the crowd.

'No more *Pomada* for you I think! Ignacio slapped him playfully him on the back.'

'*Medusas*?' Frank quickly changed the subject.

Ignacio shook his head. 'Not today.'

'Good to know.'

'Today they take a different road.' Ignacio pointed far out to sea.

The thing with Menorca was that the currents that swept around the island were often like fast flowing streams, depending on the winds and conditions out at sea. That, coupled with the shape of the many *Calas* - the long inlets that led into the smaller bays of Menorca - made it virtually impossible for the beasts to float in when currents were strong. It was equivalent to a downhill skier or Formula One driver trying to make a sudden 90-degree turn at full tilt.

However, winter storms out at sea could drive them in en masse.

Fortunately, when things were calm in the summer months, the beasts were scarce.

So, conditions were hard to predict, and were subject to change. The best evidence for lack of *Medusas* was by what you could see. Large colonies were easy to spot in the crystal clear waters on a calm and sunny day.

Today was such a day. So far. And it was usually a case of all or nothing at this time of year. The morning either yielded a clear blue vista or a red tide.

An average colony of Jelly Fish in the Med consists of hundreds of different species. Some were completely harmless.

Some, like the *Medusa,* could deliver a nasty sting.

Some, like the Portuguese Man-o-War, could inject a powerful and dangerous cocktail of poisons.

And, while it was true that the area he intended to investigate lay just beyond the mouth of the *Cala*, Frank thought it close enough for him to avoid the thoroughfare that swept the *Medusa* traffic past the bays.

After exchanging some pleasantries and jokes with the guys, he donned his wetsuit and flippers, checked that the air tank was full, enough for about 40 minutes, and strapped it on.

He then tried the demand valve, like all seasoned divers.

All seemed to be working fine.

The guys waved him off and couldn't help laughing as he made his way awkwardly due to the flippers, like some reluctant penguin, down the slipway and into the water.

Ignacio had questioned Frank's choice of a shorty wetsuit which exposed his lower arms and legs.

Sure, it was fine in the summer, but at this time of the year? Frank had said it gave him more freedom of movement, and had insisted on wearing it despite Ignacio's protestations.

He turned to José, shook his head and said 'He's gonna freeze.'

However, the water was quite warm. Except where it wasn't. Like the curates egg, the sea was 'warm in parts'. Every now and then as he made his way towards the headland of this shallow inlet he swam through a cold pocket.

That's the thing about the sea temperature around the Balearic Islands. It rarely drops below 18 degrees. Rising to a max of 25 in high summer, sometimes the air and sea temp are so close it was difficult to tell when you have actually entered the water. Not today. Mostly warm but with cold pockets.

Despite this he never failed to be enthralled by the experience of submerging, of sinking into that other sublime and silent world beneath the waves. It often made him think of the WB Yeats poem 'The Stolen Child'. One of his favourites *'Come away, O human child to the waters and the wild.'*

The muted tinkling sounds, the dappled sunlight, the warm floating sensation as if gravity existed no more, the shoals of large fish and tiny ones that swam in unison, the small brightly coloured individual fishes, deep purple anemones sprouting from rocks and sand, the kelp waving in the currents like friendly neighbours…

It was always magical, another realm where troubles and human concerns could melt up and away with the bubbles from your tank. The feeling had remained since childhood and he never tired of it.

He swam around the headland and made for the deeper water just off the mouth of Binibeca bay, carefully avoiding the notorious Juno's rocks area where many boats had historically come to grief. Too easy to lose direction in its deep canyons.

He swam over a large concrete mooring slab used by yachts to anchor so tourists could enjoy deep water snorkeling in the summer, and where the big luxury yachts of the rich could be displayed in view of, but out of reach from, the hoi-polloi.

To his disgust a large plastic sheet had lodged itself in the metal chain link on the top of the stone. It just hung there 'flapping' in the deep water like some distressed and ragged manta ray.

It always sickened him to see such man-made items polluting this exquisite environment. He determined to try and remove it at some point during this excursion. He swam on searching the seabed below him. Nothing. Perhaps he could risk just going a little further out? He checked his air gauge. 15 minutes left. Not enough to get him all the way back if he carried on, but it should be plenty if he swam back on the surface.

After a further 5 minutes, something shiny caught his eye. He swam down for a closer look. Shoes! More accurately, evening shoes!

He reached down and picked them up.

Yes, a pair of evening shoes, lying in the sand just a few feet apart. He picked them up and examined them closely. The laces were still tied.

This could explain the dead man's bare feet. But why wasn't he wearing them when they found him? How could they have come off with the laces tied?

A riddle that when solved might help to crack the whole case.

He carefully placed the footwear into the sample bag on his belt and was about to make for the surface with his prize. He froze in fear, panic rising in his stomach.

Medusas! Right in front of him, like some weird alien life form hanging in mid-air. Or in this case mid-water. He turned shoreward.

They were behind too, cutting him off from the *Cala*.

He felt a sudden sharp stinging sensation as if someone had stubbed out a cigarette on his ankle.

He whirled around. A large cloud of them were also drifting up from beneath and about to engulf him.

He kicked violently towards the surface. Only to find a thick carpet of them had drifted above him as far as he could see in all directions.

It dawned on him that this was more than just a large cluster. He had swum out too far right into a colony of huge proportions. Simply waiting for them to pass would take too long.

He checked his air gauge. Around 4 minutes worth left. Nowhere near enough to wait it out, or swim clear of this massive cloud of pain.

His mind raced. There had to be a solution. 'C'mon Think!'

The plastic sheeting! The stuff he had just been cursing. It could work!

He dove down to the stone again, through the rising horde, taking a few stings on the backs of his arms and hands, and located the man-sized block.

He pulled at the plastic sheeting and it came away easily from the rusty link. He held on to it like a man who had just found a winning lottery ticket.

He quickly spread the thick, somewhat ragged and holed plastic in front of him as best he could. It was certainly big enough to wrap around his head and shoulders. Unfortunately, his lower arms and legs were bare. He made a mental note to always wear a full-bodied wet suit with a hood on every dive from now on. If he survived this one.

He wrapped the ragged plastic sheeting tightly around his upper half, making a sort of hooded cowl for his head and face, inhaled deeply from the demand valve, unbuckled the air tank and let it fall to the sea bed, and then kicked hard for the surface.

Thanking the lord for the thoughtless idiot that had dumped this particular form of pollution into the ocean.

Gasping and crawling through the surf, he reached the shore. Despite a few stings on his arms and lower legs, the plastic sheeting had served him well, though it had been difficult to swim forwards.

The solution he soon found was to swim lying on his back, sheet wrapped tightly around him and kicking with his legs.

'*Bloody Medusas!*' He got up onto his knees facing the sea and pulled the sheeting away, a few small jellyfish falling to the sand from within its folds.

He kicked at them angrily. '*Bastards!*' But in truth he was angry with himself.

What a stupid, rookie mistake going in at this time of the year!

Turning he saw a rather bemused young couple out for a stroll along the beach with their dog.

They'd stopped to stare at this strange bedraggled fellow draped in seaweed and plastic sheeting coming out of the water and crawling along the sand.

He suddenly felt embarrassed and smiled wanly at them. '*Lo Siento.*' he mumbled as he walked unsteadily up the beach. '*Agua... peligro...medusas*'.

He heard them giggling. Felt his legs begin to buckle as the adrenaline began to wear off. Felt himself beginning to retch. Which he did. Uncontrollably.

The couple came to his assistance as he dropped to his knees. But he waved them away. ' *No es problema… estoy mareado.*'

'Perhaps you have had a brush with some *Medusas* Señor?'

He retched once more and then began to laugh.

He was still shaking as he entered his home. So much to process.

What a day it had been.

He showered which seemed to aggravate the *Medusa* stings. He treated them with an Aloe Vera gel that he kept for sunburn, put on some clean clothes and poured himself a large scotch. Downing it quickly he poured another.

He felt the pain ease and his muscles and strained nerves begin to relax. He tried to focus his mind on the findings and events of the day but his mind seemed to drift. Soon he was fast asleep in the armchair.

He dreamt that he and Linda were in a small boat in the middle of the ocean. Nothing to see but blue water in any direction. Linda frying something and preparing breakfast while he was sat at the rear fishing.

Suddenly they saw there was a storm brewing on the horizon. The boat began to rock as the storm approached and the swells grew. He felt water around his feet and saw that the boat had a leak and was quickly taking on a large amount of water. Now a glass bottom boat he could also see thousands of *Medusas* swarming beneath. He tried to warn Linda and shout to her but the wind was too loud now.

Suddenly the boat split in two under him and he felt himself fall into the morass of waiting *Medusas*.

He awoke to the sound of the phone ringing. The early morning sunlight was peeping through the slats of his Venetian blinds.

He picked it up and answered groggily. It was Juan.

'Sorry to wake you so early, but I have some news.' He sounded quite excited. 'Our pathologist has discovered some things about the body. We know the victim's identity too.'

'You were right about the assault. It's not official yet, but our forensic guys told me that the man has many broken bones, consistent with a brutal beating. It is the cause of death and he was clearly dead before he was put into the water. Robbed of his valuables as you said. In fact, all is as you said. We are very impressed here.'

Frank felt a flush of pride, which made his stings throb.

'You say you know his identity too?'

'Ah yes. It's all in the report. I am sending it to you now. I hope it will help us to track down the culprit. Well, it should give us a starting point to carry out our investigations.'

Frank saw he had a new email on his phone. 'Got it.'

'Well, I'm sure you have enough to go on to get your man now Juan. I'm glad I could help.'

Juan sounded surprised: 'No, no, Señor Frank. We are very impressed with your analysis and you must continue to act as consultant on the case. Help us solve this murder. If you would be so kind.'

He went on hurriedly. 'Of course, the department will take full credit for any successful outcomes. But your help will not go unappreciated.'

Frank hesitated. Not sure what to do. It was true he'd enjoyed the experience so far, but he was unsure if he should get involved further.

After all, he was retired. A little rusty too.

Sensing Frank's indecision Juan added 'Naturally, there will be a fee for your services.'

Well perhaps a little further then.

Just this one time.

7

SOMETHING FISHY

Shortly after breakfast the phone rang once more.

'Hello?'

'Frank, it's Charlie Mackay, how's our ace detective doing?'

'Oh, Hi Charlie. Fine... ow!' He winced as he felt stings on his hand throb as he held the receiver. 'Sorry, spilled some tea.'

Charlie chuckled. 'As long as it's not Scotch!'

He continued 'Listen, I've got some information for you about the Binibeca case. Might be somethin' or nothin'. I don't want to say too much on the phone. Why not meet me for lunch at the Triton Bar in Mahón Harbour. That's the floating one just up from the Tourist Information Centre near ya really swanky Yachts.'

Frank wondered what Charlie might have found out. Juan had already texted him some details of the victim.

His name was Ian Henderson, a retired banker from Wales. His wife had reported him missing and had come down to the police station to give details.

The description she gave seemed to fit regarding height, build and colouring, so it was then the unpleasant matter of getting her to identify the body. To spare her the gruesome and distressing task of having to see her husband's body, considering the multiple injuries and the extra insults added by the jellyfish, a certain birthmark and a distinctive scar was enough to confirm that the victim was the missing man.

He said nothing about this to Charlie when they met. He wanted to see what the man knew first.

They strolled along the paved walkway by the sea wall that skirted the Mahón Harbour road. This, the main port access road with its many seafood restaurants and souvenir shops, wound itself around the edge of the town and was always busy with cars and people.

It was also home to the many luxury Yachts that sat along the harbour wall across from the brightly canopied kerbside eateries.
As they walked Frank related his recent discovery of the shoes and close encounter with the *Medusa* colony, showing him the red scars that covered his hands like long cigarette burns.

Charlie winced visibly when he saw them. Almost everyone on the Island had had a *Medusa* sting and knew just how painful they were.

Frank's face however was also a little red but due mainly to the embarrassment he felt at making the mistake of swimming right into the pack of the nasty little beggars.

They came to the floating restaurant. Set on a large pontoon in a section between the Yacht moorings The Triton Bar was an odd affair. Not so much because it was floating, but for its eclectic and unusual mix of styles. It was part piano bar, part fish restaurant and part gentlemen's club. A bit like Rick's Place from Casablanca meets the Savoy Grill.

It was beautifully constructed in wood, like a two tier plantation house complete with wrap around upstairs balcony. Above the entrance was a carving of the sea god Triton.

As they walked to the entrance, the manager came directly out and lifting the thick rope that prevented entry by passing trade, he beamed widely as he ushered them both in.

The spacious inside was decorated with murals depicting mythical sea creatures, ornate hand-carved mirrors, chandeliers and brass rotating ceiling fans (which the place didn't need as it was well air-conditioned).

The whole thing reminded Frank of an ostentatious riverboat.

'Señor Mackay. You are looking well today. Your usual table?'

'Ay, thanks Pedro. This is Señor Harmer.'

The manager smiled ingratiatingly and led the way. He snapped his fingers and a waiter scurried over and pulled out chairs at a round table in front of a large gallery window with a magnificent view of the Harbour beyond.

The waiter presented them both with a menu, took their order for drinks and hurried off again. The host went to perform another welcome at the entrance.

Charlie looked out across the water, the sunlight glinting on the gentle waves, and sighed contentedly.

'Y'know Frank, I never tire of this view. It's not my favourite restaurant, the food is pretty braw, but the view…'

Frank looked and noticed a seagull worrying something floating in the water. It was the size of a loaf of bread and the gull was having trouble fishing it out.

'Yes. Very nice.' He was impatient to get to the matter that was on his mind. Charlie was not one to be in a hurry or to get to talk business.

It was also the Menorcan way. People first and business second.

'So, you say you have some information for me…about the body in the bay?'

Charlie made a face that looked like he had no idea what Frank was talking about and then one that said he suddenly remembered what it was. Which was not too far from the truth.

'Eh? Oh ay. That. I heard from Juan that it was a chap called Ian Henderson. He saw Frank's look of concern and surprise that he, Charlie, should already know this privileged information.

'Oh don't worry, Juan contacted me to see if I could help. Can't say I knew much about him though. Retired banker from Wales. Came over from Mallorca a few months back apparently and bought a nice little villa in Es Grau Bay, right near the *Parque Natural*.'

'That's all the official info.' He winked and put a finger to the side of his nose. 'I heard something a wee bit more useful on the island grapevine. He had a bit of a run in with someone the other night. Someone you wouldn't want to cross swords with.'

Frank waited. Charlie seemed to be trying hard to recollect something, whilst gazing at the menu as if it might be written there.

'John Dory!'

Frank was intrigued. 'John Dory? Is he another expat?'

Charlie looked at him with a puzzled frown and then burst out laughing.

'Eh? Ya numpty. No it's a fish! Best thing on the menu. Y'must try it.'

He signalled to the waiter who came and took their order. John Dory for two and a bottle of chilled *Rosado*. The waiter seemed to take a long time, much to Frank's annoyance.

When he left for the kitchen Frank asked "So… what more can you tell me? Who wouldn't you want to cross swords with?'

Charlie leant forward and spoke quietly. 'The night before he died he was seen in the company of Sir Lionel King.'

'What, *the* Sir Lionel King, the news group owner?'

'Ay, retired here in 2012. Has a big spread in the *Parque Natural*.
One of those grand edifices knocked up illegally in the 60's. That would also have made him practically neighbours with the dead chappie.'

Frank let this sink in as their aperitifs arrived with a courtesy tapas-style starter, consisting of some pieces of squid that in Frank's opinion tasted a lot better than they looked.

'Do you know Sir Lionel?' he asked.

Charlie frowned. 'Well enough to know that you wouldn't have nothing to do with him. A bad lot that one. Sure, he may be a lord of the realm now, but there's some that remember how he made his first pile with some very dodgy dealings.'

He continued. 'Had his fingers in a lot of unsavoury pies, before he got respectable. Lots of rumours about all sorts of scams and cons. Never got done for nought though. Shite never sticks to his sort.'

He sat back and shook his head ruefully. 'Gave him a Knighthood they did, but only because he stumped up a few mill in funding for the Tories. They look after their own don't they?'

Frank gave him a questioning look. All he could remember about Sir Lionel King was his pompous overbearing personality on TV chat shows and a bad Trump-esque comb-over.

Of course, he had heard rumours while he was at the Met. Sir Lionel's name had even come up in an investigation of a massive pension fund fraud, but he was never charged with anything. The man seemed to have a charmed life and obviously, friends in high places. 'The Lying King' the papers called him.

He remembered some other details from articles in the tabloids - a messy divorce, his wife citing his affairs with high-class prostitutes. It never went to court. The settlement was made quickly for an undisclosed sum.

He instinctively didn't like the man. Not just because he was crooked. He was worse than any common thief because his kind wore their aires and graces like they were superior beings. Cut from a cloth of higher moral fibre than everyone else while they lied, schemed and cheated.

Charlie continued. ' I've heard he's been into all sorts since he arrived here too. Dodgy property deals. Smuggling stuff. Never been done though. Greases all the right palms in all the right places.'

He smiled a little. 'Course, it's all petty stuff. Not a master criminal. But it just gives the place a bad name, like in the old days.'

Back in the day, like some sunnier Mediterranean climes, the Balearic Islands had always been a favourite haunt of rich expats. Those that had gained their wealth by fair means and those by foul. Some hiding from the Inland Revenue and some from the law.

Now Charlie had an angry edge to his voice and the volume of his speech increased.

'Ay, he puts on a front of respectability in public, but behind the scenes he's just another wee money grabbing shyster. We can do without his sort in Menorca.'

Charlie was proud to be an Islander, and of the many initiatives over the last few decades to rid Menorca of the bad practices and bureaucratic corruption.

In fact, he had been an instigator of change and best practice, so was not best pleased to hear of any activity that would set back Menorca's excellent modern reputation.

'Now, I'm not saying there is anything to this other business y'know.' He finished his starter and washed it down with some wine. 'I'm not saying he's involved but you have to admit it may be worth your looking into.'

Frank nodded and thanked him as the plates were cleared and their main course arrived. Sat on a big silver dish on a trolley was the largest fillet of fish Frank had ever seen. It didn't look particularly special, but it smelled exquisite.

The waiter expertly served it as Charlie looked on, nodding happily.

When he had finished he raised his glass to Frank.

'Here's to successfully sleuthing.'

Frank looked unsure and said. 'Oh I think I should leave it to the police now. After all, I am retired.'

Charlie shook his head and gave him a wry smile. 'You know what they say about old coppers don't you?'

Frank did.

8

WILD IN THE COUNTRY

Curiosity got the better of him.

As the *Parque Natural* and Sir Lionel King's place was just
a 20 minute drive from the port, he saw no harm in having a
quick look. After all, he told himself, it would be a pleasant
trip on this sunny Spring day.

He took the main road to the north of the island. After about
a mile and a half he turned off into the entrance of the
Parque Natural. As he drove along the bumpy single-track
road that led through to the coast at Es Grau, he could see
why the locals made such a fuss about this area.

The scenery was stunning, no matter where you looked.

Gently rolling hills adorned with hanging woods and lush
splashes of oleander, gorse and bracken, increased in
stature as you went.

Menorcan dry stone walls separated areas and errant stones littered the edges of footpaths. Tethered goats nibbled wild plants and grasses. Red Kites hovered and swooped.

It was all carefully unspoilt and chaotically manicured. Paradise indeed.

Commercial or domestic properties had never been officially permitted here, ever. Only agricultural buildings were allowed. Yet several large and imposing houses sat on the hillsides.

That was thanks to the unscrupulous builders and dodgy government officials back in the 60's and 70's when there was precious little actual enforcement of the planning permission rules. As long as the right bung was put in the right hands, you could build where you pleased.

In more recent years, some of these most desirable residences in this unspeakably beautiful of locations were under threat of being demolished by successive governments. Yet it never happened, though the threat was often refreshed by incoming political parties and various conservation groups, it never came to pass.

This was not so surprising as many of the properties were owned by the rich and powerful families. Some of them were in government, or had relatives in influential positions.

Who knows who you might upset dredging up the misdoings of the past. 'Best to let sleeping dogs lie' was the attitude. Kick decisions about this into the long grass and let someone else sort it out another day.

Nowadays the rules are very strictly enforced. No one gets planning permission to build anything in any area of the *Parque* except the odd footbridge or boardwalk, and even that has to meet very strict specifications.

Frank knew Sir Lionel's house as soon as he saw it, sitting at the base of a hill and backed by some dense woodland that ran right to the top.

It wasn't just the size and style that gave it away. Yes it was grand in scale with a footprint of some 1200 square metres.

Yes it was garish in appearance being a faux 17th century Menorcan country manor complete with four large peaked gable fronts, grand pillars aside a massive oak double doorway, a veranda that wrapped itself around the upper half and a clone of the Trevi Fountain complete with water feature dolphin placed right in front.

No, it was the colour. The walls and roof were painted a crimson red with cream edged lintels criss-crossing atop windows and doorways.

Charlie had said it stood out like a 'smacked arse'.

It was clearly designed to catch the eye. To say 'look at how wealthy I am' and to make passers-by wonder at the identity of such an obviously successful person.

It achieved this also by the fleet of luxury car marques parked on the massive front drive, from Bentleys to Daimlers to Ferraris all parked around the Trevi style fountain.

Frank had found cars like this to be quite rare in Menorca, many roads in the towns are narrow and there aren't many long stretches of road where a high-performance car could get out of 2nd gear. Also, he found dented vehicles seemed to be quite common on the island. Personally he'd be mortified to see his pride and joy with a dent or scratch. Menorcans weren't so precious about their cars.

They simply saw them as necessary to get them from A to B. They didn't spend each bank holiday or second Sunday valeting them like the Brits.

A beat up looking Rav 4 Jeep caught Frank's attention.

Another feature of the property stood out. Sat on the roof was a huge satellite dish and plethora of antenna and communication devices that would make NASA envious.

A huge estate surrounded the place and took in the most exuberant sea of forestry that ran from the rear of the house and up as far as the eye could see into the hills beyond.

It was a dream setting. Someone had their own woodland paradise in the heart of this nature reserve, and that someone was Sir Lionel King.

Frank drove up slowly along the gravelled drive to the large wrought iron double gates with a design of two lions standing proudly beneath a crown woven into the metalwork across the top. These sat between two imposing stone pillars. Frank noticed that these had cameras on them, one facing down at him and one along the road he had come.

He pulled up and sat there with the engine switched off, deciding whether to take a few shots with his phone, just for future reference. It always paid to have pictures. You never knew how useful they could be. Some small detail might be a big help at some point.

He got out of the car and began to take pictures with his phone. He used the zoom, as the house sat some 500 metres away.

An electronic whirring sound made him look up. The camera that was facing down began to swivel. Then in the distance near the house he heard someone shout and a car engine start. The small jeep sped towards him. It screeched to a halt, raising dust on the other side of the gates. Two burly and mean-looking men jumped out.

The smaller but nastier of the two came toward him with a threatening scowl and demanded *'Qué estás haciendo?'*

His companion, a much bigger and younger looking man, just stood by the Jeep and lit a cigarette, but never took his eyes off Frank.

Frank had met many so called 'hard men' and many genuinely frightening villains in his time. He wasn't going to be intimidated by this pair of 'rent-a-thugs'.

He smiled his most ingratiating of smiles and replied 'I saw your lovely house and just had to get a picture to take back home!'

The man almost laughed but then remembered to look threatening.

He half turned back to his partner who smirked and then spat on the ground. He then continued with contempt 'English tourist eh? Well this is off limits, not for your happy snaps. So get back in your fucking car and get the fuck out of here, fast! *Entiendes*?'

Frank resisted the temptation to reply with a short Anglo Saxon phrase. He simply smiled, nodded and got back in his car.

With a cheery wave at the two sour looking goons, who were evidently enjoying this opportunity to throw their weight around and insult a foreigner, he slowly turned the car round and then suddenly gunned the accelerator sending the wheels spinning.

This had the unfortunate effect of sending a shower of gravel over the two men.

They ducked as if it they'd been shot at. As Frank drove away he could see them in the rear view mirror waving their fists and shouting obscenities at him.

He chuckled and said 'Well you did say fast boys!'

9

BAD REPORT

'And?' There was a sour note in Sir Lionel's voice.

Immaculately dressed in cream flannel suit and club tie, he
was sat at a huge antique walnut desk, the front of which
was inlaid with two rampant lions beneath a golden crown.
He was a big man, but even if he had been a much larger
one he would have still looked dwarfed by it.

The spacious room was designed to impress. Oak panels
lined the walls. A plush green carpet patterned with gold
crowns covered the entire floor. Shelves stuffed with
important looking volumes ran the length and height of one
wall. Incongruously, several large glass tanks sat in lit
recesses, one possessing a splendid Lionfish and another a
terrarium, home to several Emperor Scorpions - both
venomous species with few predators and kings of their
domains.

His henchman stood in the doorway to the room. He looked smug as if he had done a very good job and was awaiting praise. He waited in vain and failed to sense his boss's mood and the tone.

'It was no-one. Just a nosey tourist.' He said with a dismissive wave.

'Really?' Sir Lionel got up and pointed a remote savagely at a large TV screen on a wall. It showed a freeze frame from the gate CCTV camera of Frank stood in front of his car. He zoomed in on the face.

'Well it seems this 'Tourist -' He paused and then finished his sentence with a loud menacing voice, ' - was also nosing around and examining your handiwork with the police at Binibeca yesterday!' He turned and glared at the henchman.

The man looked visibly shaken. He took a step toward the TV as if to double check the face on the screen. 'But I…he wasn't…'

'Oh he was and he is. Really, I don't know what I pay you for Miguel. You and your idiot brother. I give you both a simple job. All you had to do was go and check things out when the body turned up.'

'For goodness sake you had a clear view and you had binoculars.' He walked over to the set and waved at the screen. 'Yet you failed to recognise this fellow when you saw him again today!'

'Worse still, you have probably made him suspicious with the 'friendly' reception you gave him.'

'But he is not Menorcan police. I know them all and I do not recognise this one.' He pointed a nervous finger at the man on the screen.

'That's obvious!' Sir Lionel put down the remote, walked back to his desk and picked up a sheet of A4 paper. He waved it at the man who could see that it was some sort of printed report with a copy of an open passport on it.

'Allow me to enlighten you. He is a policeman alright. A retired detective inspector from the London Metropolitan Police. One with a reputation for solving difficult cases and catching criminals.'

Miguel looked again at the man on the screen but still failed to connect the dots. All Brits looked the same to him. He remembered seeing Inspector Juan. And yes there was someone else with him, but he just assumed it was a member of his team.

'His name is Francis Harmer. I've had our friends check him out. He's living here in Trebaluger, and right now he is helping with the case of that poor man they found in the bay.'

His anger now subsiding he decided to teach his hapless

henchman a lesson. He made a very serious face and said;

'What if that policeman comes here again? What can I say to him?'

He shook his head and said 'And to think that I have been generous enough to employ an ex-criminal with the aim to help him get back on his feet.'

Colour drained from Miguel's face and he protested ' But I was just doing what you told…'

Sir Lionel ignored this and went on 'Unfortunately, the man clearly still has criminal tendencies!'

Miguel looked horrified. 'But..but.. you told me to…'

'I told you to make sure he didn't blab to the police about our little enterprise here. Meaning you and your brother should rough him up a bit, not to kill him.'

'But, we did not mean to kill him. Just to show him we meant business. But Tomas sometimes does not know his own strength. He hit him too hard.'

Sir Lionel shook his head in mock disbelief 'One of my employees a murderer!'

Now Miguel looked truly scared.

Sir Lionel suddenly laughed a loud bray of a laugh.

Miguel forced out a feeble chuckle. He felt relieved but not amused. The bastard had been joking!

Sir Lionel sat back down at his desk.

'Relax. I'll make a call and get it taken care of.'

He picked up the phone and gestured for Miguel to leave and said firmly 'Remember, we have an important shipment to go out tonight. Check the map coordinates again. It's dark out there and it's a fishing boat we are rendezvousing with not a ferry. We don't want any more cock-ups. Do I make myself clear? '

'Si Señor King. No more cocks up.' The chastised henchman hurried out of the room.

Sir Lionel sighed and muttered to himself. 'Idiot!'

'It always pays to have powerful friends on speed-dial' he mused. Time to stop any investigation that could lead to him in its tracks. There was too much at stake to let some ex-pat English copper put a spanner in the works.

Just in case it might be worth taking out a little extra insurance. Yes, another job for Miguel and Tomás.

10

THE ROAD TO MONTE TORO

It was a bright sunny morning as Frank made his way along the Me1 towards Mercadal.

The sunlight hurt his eyes, despite his prescription sunglasses. That was no surprise really. He'd had a rotten night's sleep. He had been tossing and turning for hours, dreaming of being chased by two ferocious snarling dogs, and then falling off a dizzyingly high cliff toward jagged rocks below.

Just before dawn, he was woken suddenly by a loud banging.

It had turned windy and one of the wooden window shutters had slipped its latch and was banging against the frame with each new gust. Tired, and wanting to drift back to sleep, Frank reassured himself that the wind would soon drop and the banging would cease. But every time he was just nodding off, a fresh new gust would send the shutter crashing and jolt him back to full wakefulness.

Eventually, after what seemed like an eternity, the wind dropped and the shutter stayed still. But by then he was wide awake and, as the sun was just about to come up, he decided he might as well get up too.

He slipped out of bed and into his dressing gown. He caught his tired looking face, bedraggled hair and his bleary eyes in the dresser mirror and decided he was badly in need of a hot coffee and a cold shower.

But first order of the day? Secure that damned shutter!

He went over to the open window. In the early light he could make out most of the features of his garden and the silhouette of his car parked at the end of his driveway.

He suddenly froze and held his breath. Was that someone crouching beside his car! There was a dark shape that seemed to be moving slightly. It looked like someone was kneeling or crouching just near the front end. But it was hard to tell in this pre-dawn light. He rubbed his bleary eyes and looked again, peering hard into the gloom until his eyes began to water.

No. There was nothing there now. He shrugged and turned away figuring that it must have been the shadow of a bush moving in the breeze. Or just his imagination. Funny how your half-awake brain can play tricks on you in the half-light.

He went into the en-suite. The shower water was tepid, but he found it refreshing. Then 2 cups of black coffee and some toast later, he felt almost human again.

Then, just as he was putting the breakfast things into the dishwasher, the phone rang. He looked at the kitchen clock. It was just after 7.15. Who could be calling at this hour?

Only one way to find out. He picked up the receiver.

But when he answered there was only silence. He sensed that there was someone at the other end and he thought he heard breathing, but after a few minutes concluded it was one of those annoying automated sales calls and went to put the phone down. It was then he heard the voice.

It was a man's voice. With a strange accent, almost as if he was trying to decide what to say, or to disguise his real voice. 'Señor Harmer? Are you there?'

The tone was flat and emotionless. But there was something vaguely familiar about it. Frank answered. 'Yes. Who's this?'

The caller would not give his name but said that he had some very important information regarding the man in Binibeca bay!

When Frank enquired for more, the man said that he felt it was not safe to speak on the phone, and would prefer to meet him and tell him in person, somewhere out quiet. He suggested that they meet in the car park at the top of Monte Toro.

Frank was intrigued. Firstly, because this might be a genuine informant. Perhaps he had witnessed the killing, or at least knew someone that had. Secondly, how did the man have his number? Or even know he was involved in the case? Perhaps the man would want money for his secrets. Well, there was nothing for it but to meet the fellow and ask him, he concluded.

He agreed to the meeting and the man hung up abruptly.

So here he was driving to the central Menorcan town of Es Mercadal and then 2 miles on to take the steep road that led to the top of Monte Toro.

Rising to a height of 1175 feet, Monte Toro, or El Toro as it is known locally, is the tallest hill on the island. Many islanders regard it as the spiritual centre of Menorca and the summit is home to the Sanctuary of the Virgen del Toro, an old Gothic church dating from 1670 when Augustinian monks established a monastery there. Legend says that a bull led the monks to a statue of the Virgin Mary carved in the rock face. Hence the name El Toro.

Nowadays, the sanctuary is inhabited by a religious community of Franciscan nuns. It is open to the public, and popular with tourists all year round, featuring a small chapel, a gift shop, café, and a wooden carved figure of the Toro Virgin (Menorca's patron Saint).

In front of the gates to the sanctuary stands the imposing statue of 'Jesus of the Sacred Heart', his arms outstretched to bless the Menorcans who died in the Spanish Moroccan wars of the early 20th century.

From Monte Toro you have breathtaking views of the whole of the island, from Ciutadella to Fornells. It is said that on a clear day you can even see the mountains of Mallorca.

But the road to the top is narrow, winding, and in parts treacherous. Drivers up and down must take extreme care, especially on the bends where there is little more than a short dry-stone wall to stop you from going over the edge and tumbling down to your doom.

Frank was not normally a nervous driver. Though the road is easily a 1 in 10 gradient, he was not too apprehensive about the drive up. It was the drive down he wasn't looking forward to.

The last time he had been taking it slow and steady on the descent, but the other drivers didn't seem to share his trepidation and he had some very scary near misses on some of the bends and narrower stretches. Still, today he could not let such things bother him. Today he had a rendezvous at the top that might give him and Juan the lead that they needed to crack the case.

The final bend at the top of the hill was the steepest. It swept up between grassy slopes that hid the summit from view until you crested the top. You were immediately greeted by the towering statute of Jesus with his arms outstretched as if in welcome, and the charming whitewashed outer walls of the enclave. It reminded Frank of an old Mexican mission he had seen in a cowboy movie.

He pulled into the car park. It was still on the early side for visitors, so there were only a few other vehicles. There were a couple of service and delivery vans, some cars belonging to the visitor centre staff, and the few early bird visitors. None of them seemed to be occupied.

No sign of anyone. He sat and waited. And waited. He checked his phone for messages. And waited. Listened to the radio. Ate a few jelly babies – he always kept his glove compartment well-stocked with them. And waited.

After half an hour he got out to stretch his legs. The bad one always seemed to seize up and cramp if he sat still for too long. He took in the view.

From here the view of the south of the island was incredible, marred only by a collection of communication masts, planted around the hilltop like some scaled down Eiffel towers and bristling with aerials and dishes and other communication technology.

It was a smashing day. As clear as you could wish for. The bright sun bounced off the sea in the distance and yes, he shaded his eyes with his hand, you could just pick out the mountains of North East Mallorca in the distance. That would be the coastline of Pollença if he'd got his geography right. It was supposed to be the nicest and greenest part of the island, quite beautiful and a lot like Menorca they say. He planned to get the ferry over there one day and take a look for himself.

He looked at his watch and saw that more than an hour had past since his arrival. It was getting hot up here and he was feeling hungry, and annoyed. It looked like the guy was going to be a no show. Bloody time waster!

He looked around the car park once more, trying to see if any of the vehicles were occupied. But then, the guy would surely have approached or signaled to him by now if he was there. He had insisted Frank be there by 10.30, and said he had to be there on time and would not wait.

Well, Frank had waited long enough and decided to head back home.

He remembered that the first bend was bad. But the second was even worse. Talk about a 180! The teetering drop was just inches from your offside wheels! It made Frank's stomach loop de loop just to think of it.

If you went over the edge there, the only thing between you and the floor of the valley far below was the old dry-stone wall, barely a metre in height. Not much of a safety barrier, Frank thought grimly. He wondered why the authorities hadn't bothered to put anything more substantial in place.

He smiled as he recalled the John Denver ditty about a town with a treacherous mountain road, where there had been many fatal accidents with vehicles going over the edge, at a viewing point on a bend. The town council had not wanted to spoil the view for the tourists, so instead of installing a safety barrier they decided to put an '*ambulance down in the valley*'.

He always found the thought amusing. But not today strangely enough.

He drove carefully over the brow and down the first steep incline, hugging the hillside on his right as he crawled around the tight curve at the bend. Despite his concentration he couldn't help but admire the view. The whole of southern Menorca was spread out in front of him like a feast of glorious treats on a giant sun-dappled picnic blanket.

The next bit was a narrow straight that led directly to a hairpin. The one that Frank always dreaded.

The car was picking up speed now. He pressed the brake pedal to maintain a steady pace. It felt a little spongey and the brakes didn't seem to be as responsive as usual. The car wasn't slowing down quite enough to take the bend comfortably.

He pressed a little harder, but it had no noticeable effect. He felt panic rising. He was almost at the bend now and going much too fast. He pressed hard on the brakes this time. There was a slight resistance, then a clunking sound as the pedal went right down to the floor with no effect. Now he had no brakes at all!

It took all of his concentration to ride the curve, fighting the centrifugal force that was trying to tip the car over, scraping along the inside of the small wall, the yawning drop on the other side.

Then suddenly he was through the bend and onto the next straight. The car whipped along gaining even more speed. He thought about using the handbrake but at this speed it might spin or flip the car. It was also impossible to change down the gears to slow the car.

The vehicle kept on gaining speed as it hurtled toward the next bend. It was another hairpin.

But this time, thankfully, it was a left hand curve, which would mean he would be hugging the hillside and not skirting the drop. Still. He could not risk losing control and skidding across the road. There was no way at this speed that the wall would be able to save him.

The main thing was to get around this bend in one piece and then he could probably make it down the rest of the hill, which was less steep with fewer and much kinder bends. He would just have to ride it out.

Luckily he had been in enough hairy car chases to know how to handle a vehicle at high speeds in unsafe conditions. Yes. The road was narrow, and he needed all the room, and luck, that he could get.

But it would work out as long as he didn't meet any vehicles coming the other way.

Shit! A minibus was just rounding the bend and taking up most of the road. Schools often brought classes up to visit the sanctuary, so it would no doubt be full of kids. He needed to think fast.

There was no way he could stop, and no way he could get past the bus. It sat in the middle of the road with a small space on either side. It was enough for a motorbike perhaps. But not a car. He knew he couldn't risk a head on collision. Not with a bus full of children!

There was just a chance he could squeak through on the hillside flank of the bus if the driver would pull over nearer to the wall.

He flashed his lights repeatedly. The bus driver took a second and then seemed to realise they were in immediate danger, especially as Frank was waving his arms, telling him to move over. They were just a few yards apart and collision now seemed inevitable.

Frank could see him turn the steering wheel frantically and the bus began to veer to the left. It didn't look like he would make it in time and the gap wasn't growing fast enough. But he had no choice but to drive for it anyway. He braced for impact and gripped the wheel with all of his might to hold the car steady.

There was an ear-piercing screeching of metalwork as the car's wheels dropped into a deep drainage ditch on one side, and scraped along the length of the bus on the other.

Frank was buffeted about like a rag doll as unforgiving concrete blocks and metal drain covers did untold damage to the underside of his car. Still, he had avoided the crash.

The car began to slow a little as it grounded on the concrete edge of the ditch. Then it stopped suddenly and Frank was jerked forward, his head dipping and hitting the steering wheel just before the Airbag deployed and slapped him hard in the face.

He sat there for several moments feeling dazed, then elated at the realization that he had survived and was still in one piece. Even if his car wasn't.

Crash avoided. He was glad he had paid attention in those police advanced driving classes, and thankful for the quick reflexes of the school bus driver.

The bus had stopped too and, from the angle he was pitched at he could just see the children on the bus staring down at him through its windows, looking shocked and scared.

He smiled awkwardly and gave them a thumbs up.

They waved back and smiled. He began to laugh. As much in relief as anything. Now all he had to do was get out of this ditch. This wonderful ditch. They were quite commonplace around the island and the cause of many a hire car being damaged, usually by an unwary tourist. He always thought they were a bad idea.

He never thought he would actually be glad to have driven into one.

When the breakdown vehicle arrived, Frank described what had happened to the man from the garage. He said it was probably a leak in the brake fluid, caused by a broken pipe or a worn seal. They would check it out in their workshop and let him know the cause, but he was sure that however it happened it was just a case of bad luck.

Frank wasn't so sure. He had the feeling that 'bad luck' may have had a helping hand or two.

11

DINNER DATE

He picked up a hire car in Mercadal and on his way home
called at the Supermercado in Trebaluger to pick up some
steak for his dinner. It was the only store in this small
urbanization and as such was always busy.

It was not a large place, just four main aisles crammed with
every conceivable convenience product, a chilled section
for fresh food, a long open top freezer packed with a variety
of frozen meat and fish, and a fruit and veg section at the
far end next to the drinks section.

It was located just after the turn into Trebaluger from the
San Luis road and was a100 yards or so from Frank's
home. He could see it from his front gate.

As he entered the store he got a few strange looks from
some of the staff. They knew him and nodded in greeting,
but it was clear they also noticed the sticking plaster on his
forehead and the swelling around his left eye, now turning
an unpleasant shade of blue.

He was weighing out some large lemons when he heard a familiar voice.

'How is the investigation going Señor Harmer?'

Marisol. What were the odds? She must have come in to the store just behind him. He turned and she did a small double take when she saw his facial injuries. She decided not to mention it, just in case it would embarrass him. He decided not to mention his harrowing expedition to Monte Toro. Later maybe.

"Oh Hi Marisol. Well I'm not really working on it. Just helping the police with their 'enquiries.'

Some nearby shoppers, other local ex-pats stared on hearing this. To Brits helping the police with their enquiries' was a euphemism for being arrested for a crime.

She came over and examined the grapefruits. 'Well I am sure they appreciate it.' She put some into a bag and weighed it. Printed out a ticket and stuck it into a shopping basket.

The ex-pats had edged closer and were pretending not to be listening. She noticed this and, smirking, spoke in a low voice 'So, have you found out who is the murderer of poor Señor Henderson?'

He looked at her in amazement, did everyone on this bloody island know? He shook his head and had to laugh.

The ex-pats looked transfixed. He thought it best to downplay things.

'Well, I think the police have some leads but I'm not sure if there's much to go on yet.'

Marisol looked a little disappointed. Then brightened. 'Perhaps I could help you to examine the evidence. After all, I know the island well. And maybe I have some experience of the law, yes?

It was true, she could be a real help here. She clearly had an ear to the island grapevine, and her job gave her access to all sorts of information. She might know a thing or two about the goings on where Sir Lionel King was involved.

The ex-pats were clearly intrigued now. He thought it best to draw this to a conclusion and get out of the store as quickly as possible.

'Why don't we discuss it over dinner?' 'My place?'

Damn. Where did that come from?

Marisol's smile was like the dawn breaking on a bright summer morning. She sounded a little surprised but delighted. 'Ah, it would be my pleasure. I will bring wine. And perhaps you should get an extra steak.'

He looked at her quizzically.

She laughed and said 'One for your eye!'

She skipped to the till with her shopping, chattering to him as she did so. He didn't hear a word.

What was he doing? Fool! She might think he was interested in her. He suddenly realised that perhaps he was.

12

BAD NEWS

While he was preparing the meal, Frank's house phone rang.

'Hello, Señor Harmer?'

It was Juan.

'Hi Juan. How are you? Did you get my message. I left the shoes I found with your desk sergeant.'

There was a brief pause and then Juan answered. 'Er, yes. Sure. Thank you.' Here he hesitated as if not knowing how to continue. 'But I have some bad news for you. I have been called off the case.' He sounded more than a little embarrassed by this revelation.

'What? But I thought we had a strong lead here. What about Sir Lionel? Isn't he a person of interest?'

'Well, that is my opinion, of course. But he is also a good friend of some people in some very high places.

Frank said 'I see.' But didn't.

'Yes. I have been told to forget the whole thing. That this is obviously an unfortunate accident, and that is what it will now be saying in the pathologist's report.'

Frank felt himself getting angry. 'Now hold on Inspector. There was evidence to suggest foul play here. The findings by your lab guys, they said it was clear he was beaten.'

'A mistake. Now they think the injuries are more likely to be consistent with a fall from a boat onto some rocks. He hesitated and then said flatly. 'And the personal effects simply washed off by strong currents.'

Juan was not very convincing. It didn't sound like he really believed in what he was saying, but realised the man was reluctantly obeying his superiors. Clearly, someone didn't want this to be a murder. Was it political or just to avoid bad press. Or something more sinister?

Frank heard him sigh heavily. 'So I will not be able to investigate this matter further.'

Frank was dumbfounded. He didn't quite know how to respond to this.

He felt especially frustrated now that there was a lead and the case seemed to be getting somewhere. His coppers nose told him there was something in it and it was much more than just an 'accident'.

He was about to slam the phone down when he heard Juan say 'I said *I* will not be able to investigate this matter further. But then I must obey and answer to my superiors.' He paused. 'You however...'

Frank smiled suddenly and said. 'D'you know. I was thinking of revisiting the *Parque Natural* again soon. Think I spotted a very interesting species worthy of closer examination.'

'Well,' there was a chuckle in Juan's voice. 'Better keep a low profile. You would not want to scare this creature away!'

Then added. 'By the way, the shoes were several sizes too big for Mr Henderson. Very strange, do you not think?'

Frank did.

13

THE 'RECKIE'

They walked cautiously and as stealthily as possible through the dense woodland that ran down the hill to the rear of Casa Lionel. The whisper of the wind through the pines was quite eerie. Bracken and dried twigs crackled beneath their feet occasionally and made Marisol giggle.

Frank cursed himself for letting her talk him into coming on this night reckie. How unprofessional of him. How stupid to let her do so knowing that she'd had quite a few glasses of wine. She seemed to be treating the whole thing like a party game. Not the serious and perhaps dangerous stake-out it might turn out to be, given his previous reception.

She'd persuaded him with her knowledge of the area, saying that she had played here as a child and been on many walking trips through the park to study rare and endangered plants and wildlife. Now he felt that they also might become two of these.

Suddenly a torchlight beam split the dark, coming from the top of the ridge behind them from where they had already walked down.

It made a sweep through the trees in their direction.

He instinctively grabbed Marisol and pulled her down to the ground with him. He pulled a little too hard and Marisol ended up crashing forward on her hands and knees. Unaware of the danger she misinterpreted this move and laughing said. 'Oh, Señor Frank!'

He put his hand to her mouth and shushed her. But too late. The torch beam now stopped and then was pointed in their direction.

Shit! Frank held his breath. Marisol, now realising that something serious was happening remained still and gave him a frightened questioning look.

Clearly, she hadn't seen the torch light, but now realised that they were not alone, and in danger of been caught by one of Sir Lionel's minders that Frank had told her about.

Frank recognised Miguel's gruff voice immediately.

'¿Hola? ¿Quién está? ¿Eres tú Tomás? ¿No me jodas eh?

They remained still. Not daring to breath as the torchlight fretted among the bushes where they hid. It stopped suddenly and the torch holder dropped the thing as it startled a screech owl, which, not impressed, let out a piercing screech that echoed for miles in the still night air as it flew away.

After a few moments the shock wore off and Miguel retrieved his torch, muttering words that Frank could tell were not singing the owl's praises. Sir Lionel's man then lit a cigarette to calm his shattered nerves and walked off along the ridge to check the perimeter fence.

Frank thanked his lucky stars and the owl and hoped that the man would walk in the opposite direction from where they had broken through the fence to gain entry.

He nodded to Marisol that it was okay to get up now and that the danger had passed. They smiled smiles of relief and then, making sure the man and his torch had moved well away, continued on their journey down towards the low buildings to the rear of the main house.

Strangely his leg wasn't bothering him at all, despite the steep incline and uneven terrain. He put it down to adrenaline. Or maybe it was just plain old fear.

Either way, he wasn't sure whether they were doing the smartest thing any more. All he knew was he was feeling more alive and enjoying this adventure more than anything that he had done for a long, long time.

He just hoped it wasn't all going to end in tears.

Or worse.

14

ON THE BEACH AT SUNSET

Juan Diego Rodriguez, Inspector de Policia in Mahón
walked slowly along the water's edge at Son Bou, the sun
low on the horizon.

It was his favourite beach on the island and his favourite
time of day. It helped him to think, to clear his mind.

Where it was true that there were many other, perhaps more
secluded beaches to choose from like Macarelleta or Cala
Mitjana, none in his opinion offered the scenic splendour of
this one.

It was a mile-long strip of white sand and, behind it one of
the prettiest hillsides in Menorca adorned with holiday
villas dotted among well-manicured avenues adorned with
pine trees.

He often came here to walk and think. To clear his mind or resolve a difficult problem. Like the one he was wrestling with now.

How could he let the man down like this? This icon that he held in great esteem. What would he think? Especially as Señor Harmer had seen the evidence with his own eyes and made his own, and most likely accurate conclusions.

Now it would seem that he, Juan, was either incompetent or that there was something fishy going on and that he was part of it.

How else could it look? Even he suspected that someone on high had pulled a few strings. Got the pathology department to change their minds. 'A tragic boating accident.'

He'd often heard that there was some 'old boys' network as the British say, a remnant of the 'old days'. What is it that they say 'Power Corrupts?'

He'd seen this kind of thing happen before and a few of his colleagues divulged that they had received similar instructions from on high. 'The case is now closed. Let it go now'. 'Forget it. It's in your own interest.'

But was it though? Yes, it would be so easy to walk away. Yet they'd been on to something. His gut told him so.

Someone got scared and had the clout to get the plug pulled, and no prizes for guessing who that someone was.

His train of thought was suddenly interrupted, as he had to stop to negotiate a large mound of seaweed that had been piled up at the water's edge. This was a common practice on beaches in Menorca during the non-tourist seasons and winter months. The seaweed was regularly gathered and stored, and then used to form a barrier against storm erosion.

He looked out to sea, lit a fresh cigarette and returned to the internal debate.

This sort of mild corruption was supposed to have been stamped out years ago. But of course, in every walk of life, every kind of business, you still got the occasional bad apple.

The police force was no more immune to it than banks or political parties. He watched the waves break and the white foam of the surf wash up to where he was standing, wetting his feet, his shoes safely tucked into his jacket pockets.

Yes, he could make waves. Question the changed pathology report and push for a re-examination.

On the other hand, he was comfortable in a well-paid job, loved his work and the people he worked with and loved this island, so different from the world he had left behind in Spain's capital city. No major crime here. No gang warfare. No drug runners or racketeers. Well, that wasn't quite true if you count people like Sir Lionel and yes, there was the occasional robbery, assault and sometimes murder to solve.

But compared to the mainland this place was like *Hobbiton*.

So why rock the boat and risk everything he had worked for?

He felt himself getting angry.

Why? Because, despite living the good life, he was still a cop.
A really good one like his older brother Francisco had been. He had died responding to a robbery gone-bad.

He remembered his brother's face the last time they had talked in that little bar in Madrid, just off the Plaza Mayor. He remembered how they had joked about who was the best cop and who would make it to the top first.

Francisco never had the chance. Those scumbags made sure of that.

He recalled some of Francisco's favourite sayings 'If you're going to be a cop, be a good one.' And 'It's our job to enforce the law, no fear no favour.'

He then realised why he had looked up so much to Frank Harmer. Aside from the similar Christian name, and the fact that Francisco would be about Frank's age now had he survived, it was that the hostage drama where Frank was shot – it had been all over the news a short time after Francisco's death.

He remembered reading all about it and about Frank's heroism at the time. He had made a connection and Frank had become an older brother figure to him.

It helped somehow to know that someone had bravely faced danger and survived. Had risked his life by putting others first.
Just like Francisco had.

He stood there a while longer. The sun was almost touching the horizon, turning the sea golden. Tears stung his eyes. He flicked the cigarette into the water.

No! This shit was not going to go down. Not if he could help it.

Then a worrying thought occurred to him. If someone had the power to quash this investigation, someone who was clearly involved in a brutal murder, Frank Harmer may be walking into danger right now.

He ran barefoot back to his car. His shoes falling to the sand where the sea would claim them later that evening.

15

IN THE LION'S DEN

As they got nearer, the woodland was less dense and they began to see what they at first thought were houselights. No, not houselights but window lights from some very large but low warehouse type building completely hidden from view from all but this vantage point.

Marisol was clearly sober now and more than a little concerned for their safety. She had been badly shaken by the events near the ridge and suggested that perhaps they should come back another time. Preferably in the daylight. Preferably armed and with a large dog.

Frank was inclined to agree and was about to stop the mission when he saw the lights, just over a lower ridge that hid most of the rear of property from view.

What was this large building for? Why were all the lights on? Come to think of it, why was there a security patrol at night? What was going on in this place that was so precious that it needed a night guard?

He had to find out.

Just a little closer. Perhaps he could get a look through one of the building's windows.

Marisol pulled at his elbow as he went to move forward.

'Look, I just want a quick peek at what's going on in there and then we can go. You just wait here and I'll be two minutes.'

She didn't look too convinced but reluctantly agreed. 'Okay. Two minutes and then we vamos, yes?'

He smiled and squeezed her a hand. It was shaking a little. Perhaps adrenaline or the chill of the night air. It was a crazy time to notice but in the glow of the moonlight her upturned face looked radiant. Her eyes wide and enchanting. Was he falling for her? It had been 4 years since he'd lost his wife and in that time had not even looked at another woman.

His train of thought was suddenly interrupted as his phone vibrated for the 4th time that evening and made him jump. He was glad he had turned off the sound, but still.

He let it go to voicemail just as he did with the previous three calls.

He squeezed her hand again and, with a crouching gait, moved out from the cover of the trees. She watched his shrinking silhouette approach the large building in short stealthy movements. She sat down on her haunches and smiled to herself. 'Men!'

Now she felt the cold night air and shivered. She suddenly sensed someone approaching from behind and half turned to see a shadowy figure brandishing a weapon of some kind.

Her scream was stifled as a rough hand was clamped over her mouth.

Frank heard nothing and was focused on what was inside this large wooden warehouse.

He rubbed at the dusty and partially obscured windowpane and was perplexed at what he saw.

Rows of trestle tables sat beneath dim strip lights. But where he expected to see Marihuana growing in hydroponic trays, there were clear-sided plastic boxes filled with colourful flowers and what looked like animal transporting crates in which he could just make out creatures about the size of rabbits.

Not all the crates and boxes had plants or animals in them. But he could see there were at least a dozen that did.

What the…? This was hardly the big secret he was expecting to find. Not the drug factory, the money forging or slave trafficking.

Some plants and bunnies? What was Sir Lionel doing with…

The blow came but he was unconscious before the pain could register.

The room was moving. Back and forth, up and down and around and around.

There was a humming sound and a smell Frank knew very well.

Blood. In his nostrils and pain in the left side of his head. He opened his eyes, the bright light hurt and made them water. He blinked this away and the room came into focus, slowly.

The moving room now made sense. He was on a yacht. A rather large and splendid one judging by the luxury interior of this cabin.

He tried to sit, but found it difficult with his hands tied behind him with a cable tie.

He managed to shuffle into an upright sitting position and saw that he was sat on a well-upholstered sofa with Marisol slumped unconscious beside him and similarly bound.

He could see she was alive and breathing, no sign of injury so most likely she had been drugged.

It made him angry. After all, he was a copper and he'd been here before. She on the other hand was an innocent and they had no right to manhandle her this way. He would make them pay, but decided to hold his ire in check. For now.

Sat across from them in a swivel chair and with his back to them sat Sir Lionel. He turned to face them with a huge grin on his face.

'Ah, I see you have decided to join us. I hope we haven't made you too uncomfortable.'

Frank attempted a sardonic smile but winced instead as he felt a fresh stab of searing pain in his temple.

'Sorry about the rough stuff. Tomás can be a trifle over-zealous in his work as you may have already gathered. I'll get you something for that in a moment. But first I expect you are a little curious as to what exactly is going on?'

Frank decided that Sir Lionel was clearly insane so that it would be best to play along and humour him.

He cleared his throat, forced a wry smile and said.' Well it had crossed my mind, what with all the plants and bunnies. Are you opening some sort of petting zoo?'

Sir Lionel frowned and then let out a huge raucous laugh. 'Petting Zoo! Hah. That's good. Did you hear that? Opening a Petting Zoo!'

Frank heard someone laughing behind him and realized that one of Sir Lionel's goons must also be in the room, suitably armed no doubt. It would probably be Dumber, as Dumb would be driving the boat.

Sir Lionel carried on. 'No. no. What you saw were not bunnies and flowers. Our cargo is far more precious than that.'

He stood and strutted around as he talked, like a school master delivering a lecture to a class of young children.

"The Dragon Mouth Lily and the Black Lizard are both indigenous to the island of Menorca.' He turned to see if Frank was paying attention.

Frank gave him a 'so what' look.

He smiled and went on. 'Not only that, they are extremely rare. In fact, there is only one place on the entire planet that both of these specimens are found.'

'That's right. Menorca. And that makes them a very valuable commodity.'

Frank said. 'You are smuggling flowers and geckos?'

Sir Lionel stared at him for a few seconds, trying to decide if Frank was goading him or was actually clueless. He decided perhaps it was the latter and thought it best to break this down for the copper. Besides he loved a captive audience and hadn't done any public speaking for a long time.

'Transience, my dear Mister Harmer is a commodity that makes some things desirable. A fleeting beauty to be treasured for its own sake despite there being no residual value.'

He walked over to a cabinet just at the edge of Frank's field of vision and returned with a small wooden case the size of a shoebox. He then opened the lid and very carefully, almost lovingly removed a small plant with a long green stem and small white petals.

He held it up and spoke. 'This single specimen will fetch me over 10,000 euros.' The look on his face was sheer delight. 'Exquisite is it not?'

Frank thought the plant was rather ordinary looking, but he thought the sums were impressive.

'And the Black Lizard?' he asked.

'Ah, so you were paying attention. The Black Lizard will fetch even more. Upwards of 25,000 euros. Some buyers will pay even more if I can get a bidding war going.'

Frank knew his next question was pointless but he had to ask it anyway. His head was clearing now and he needed time to think if he and Marisol were going to get out of this in one piece. No doubt Sir Lionel wasn't taking them on this boat ride for fun.

'But aren't they both protected species. Isn't it against the law to take them off the island?'

Sir Lionel put the plant gently back into its container. He sat back down in the swivel chair and chuckled, shaking his head from side to side.

'I am merely a businessman utilising a natural resource. I provide collectors with items that otherwise would be impossible to obtain via conventional conduits, circumnavigating the red tape and petty regulations of the port authorities.'

'You could say that I am providing an essential service.'

During this speech he felt a hand squeeze his thigh twice. Marisol! She was awake but clearly pretending to be out cold. She must have heard what was going on and realised the danger they were both in.

She slumped against him and groaned, still pretending to be out of it.

Then, behind him, he felt something small and sharp being placed into his hands. The shark tooth pendant!

He decided to stall a bit more. Humour the mad bugger until he could form a plan and cut through his bonds. He smirked and said 'So. In other words you are just a common smuggler.'

At this Sir Lionel glared and said angrily 'Stupid Biosphere Reserve! So what if I take a few plants and creatures? They grow in my back yard for Heaven's sake. The *Parque Natural* has plenty. They have been growing and breeding here for decades. There's plenty to go around.'

'Well, I doubt the authorities will see it that way. There's stiff penalties for smuggling protected flora and fauna. Prison no doubt. Especially as you've killed to protect your activities from discovery.'

This last shot got Sir Lionel back on his feet. He snapped his fingers at his henchman and said.

'In that case I had better make sure I'm not found out, hadn't I?'

Frank heard the goon stir himself and he loomed into view brandishing a pistol. He needed more time and said 'But what about the evening clothes?'

Sir Lionel looked puzzled and then realised Frank was referring to the DJ that the man in the bay was wearing when he was discovered.'

'Ah. A subterfuge. To throw the local bobbies off the sent. Dressed like that they would naturally conclude that he had been at some posh dinner on a Yacht and fallen into the water. So we dressed him up in one of my DJ's. Trouble was he was a darn sight smaller than me but who would really notice that after the sea and fishes had their sport?'

Frank looked down at the big man's feet and nodding said 'That explains the shoes then. They must have slipped off the victim quite easily when they became waterlogged.'

Tomás, grinning, loomed over them pointing the gun. He nodded towards the door.

'What? You're going to kill us too? That's not going to look too clever. You're already a suspect. You'll be found out.'

Sir Lionel grinned smugly. 'Oh I very much doubt that. Boating accidents happen all the time. These Yacht owners are terrible drink drivers!'

'Tomás. See our guests to their new quarters. ' Make them as uncomfortable as possible and give them a good send off.'

The man seemed confused.

Sir Lionel sighed 'Take them to the back of the boat and cast them adrift in the dingy you fool.'

He got up from his chair and opened the door for them. He followed them out 'I'd better take the helm from here. We have to go slow while you launch the dingy and I'm not sure we can trust your brother to keep us on an even keel with these swells. I'll send him back to help you with them.'

The two henchmen led them to the rear of the craft while Sir Lionel took the helm and slowed the vessel down. They were now out at sea and in the pitch dark, except for the cabin lights of the Yacht and the occasional distant sweep of the Faro de Favaritx lighthouse.

The two burly men bundled them into a small boat that was tethered just behind the low rear deck at the back yacht.

Marisol now fully awake had made her own protests and used a few choice words that even Miguel was shocked by. But she realised that perhaps playing along might be their best chance of escape.

Stall for time while Frank worked on cutting the cable tie. She wasn't sure what they would do then, but one problem at a time.

Sir Lionel's plan was to cast the dingy adrift as the Yacht moved slowly forward, then come about from a suitable distance bearing down on it at full speed, sinking it and the occupants, who if not killed by the impact would never survive out here all night.

Of course, foul play would be suspected if they were found with their hands tied behind them. So Miguel was instructed to inflict the necessary injuries and remove the cable ties from their unconscious bodies before setting them adrift in the small boat.

Satisfied that they had it all under control, victims secured in the dingy, brains about to be bashed in, Miguel sent his brother to report the status to Sir Lionel who could then get the boat going forward and ready to make its 'accident' run.

They sat there looking up at the remaining henchman, their little craft bobbing about cheerily in the choppy water.

Miguel, standing just above them on the aft deck, now held what looked like a metal baseball bat. He waved it at them and with a sour grin said 'Okay. Now it is time for lights out. So who wants to be first?'

They glared up at him in stony silence.

Thanks to the bobbing movement of the boat Frank was able to hide the busy sawing motion behind him as he cut at the bonds with the shark tooth. He'd inflicted quite some damage to his wrists in the process but managed to avoid slicing through an artery.

Another moment or two and he would be through it.

'No-one?' Miguel sighed dramatically and shook his head. 'You English. So reserved.' He raised the bat above his head with both hands, taking aim at Frank's head. 'The gentleman I think.'

Marisol realised Frank needed more time.

She sneered at the lumbering figure. 'Oh, you are the big man when it comes to hitting defenceless women, yes? Yet you run around for your boss like a small child. You…you little man!'

Miguel looked stunned, lowered the bat slightly, then laughed. 'Hah. This one has spirit. More than I can say for you English.'

'Perhaps I finish the bitch off first after all.'

He raised the bat once more, now taking aim at Marisol.

'Now it's time to say goodnurrghh..!

The fist in the solar plexus took the wind out of him. He dropped to his knees just as a head butt caught him full in the face, breaking his nose and dislodging several teeth.

Before he could scream for help, the bat now in Marisol's capable hands knocked him out cold with one savage hit. Frank was impressed, she had already cut though her own tie and had hidden the fact well.

They clambered onto the aft deck and then shoved his limp, unconscious body into the boat, which they then cast adrift.

As they were untying it from the cleats Frank gave Marisol an admiring grin. 'Remind me not to play poker or rounders with you.'

She laughed. 'A baseball-mad Father and card-playing Mother taught me everything I know.'

Then, seeing a figure approaching from the front of the Yacht along the narrow gangway that ran along the side of the vessel, she quickly put a finger to her lips.

They crouched in the semi-darkness, staying quiet and still. They heard the voice of Sir Lionel. He sounded impatient.

'Is it done yet? Hurry up Miguel I can't leave your idiot brother steering for long.'

No answer came from the rear. He came closer, his eyes searching the darkness. Seeing the boat drifting away he barked at the huddled shape in the darkness. 'Miguel? What are you waiting for? Is there a problem?'

Frank stood and then Marisol. 'Sorry Sir Lionel. Miguel can't hear you on account of him not being here.'

Marisol added 'He had a headache and went for a lie down.'

Sir Lionel said nothing for a moment as he tried to take in what had happened. Then he yelled for Tomás at the top of his voice as he hurried forward.

Unfortunately, Miguel's brother was no sailor and the boat yawed violently to one side as it hit a swell, tipping his boss onto the side rail.

He grabbed at it and hung on briefly until another swell staggered the boat violently.

He pitched head first into the water.

Not a strong swimmer he floundered in the choppy waters and was dragged under momentarily in the big boat's wake. He came up spluttering and cursing as they watched him disappear into the night.

Hearing his boss's shouts, Tomás cut the engines and went to see what was going on. Wary, he crept forward toward the aft deck with his gun in his hand.

Just then two powerful search lights and a blaring ships horn were enough to stop him in his tracks. He whirled around to see the shape of a police launch sail into view at speed. Seizing the opportunity, it didn't take more than a sharp blow with the bat and a good shove to put him over the side too.

The police launch slowed and came alongside. Several armed policemen in uniform stood on its deck, and in plain clothes Inspector Juan Diego Rodriguez. He had a quizzical look on his face but was clearly happy to see them.

He cupped his hands and shouted 'You're having a busy night my friends!'

Frank and Marisol waved to him and Frank shouted back 'Nothing we can't handle! I think you'll find some very interesting cargo on here. Enough to put our Knighted friend and his pals away for a few years, never mind the murder.'

He pointed into the dark 'There's two of them in the water and another somewhere back there in a dingy.'

He added 'Got a nasty bump on his head!'

Juan laughed. Frank and Marisol giggled like two teenagers.

The officers fished the bedraggled villains out of the water.

Frank was curious to know how Juan had found them and come to their aid so quickly. He shouted across to him 'How did you find us out here?'

Juan reached into his jacket pocket and took out his mobile phone. He held it up so Frank could see 'GPS. We tracked your phone to Sir Lionel's hacienda and there we found some very interesting and illegal going's on. They were also kind enough to leave a map for tonight's little rendezvous. But now it will be us that will be turning up to meet their partners in crime.'

Juan looked down at the two soaking wet men coughing and spluttering on the deck of the launch.

He spoke to his men who then led them roughly away, then he turned back to Frank and Marisol.

'These fish will give us all the information we need, that is if they want us to go easy on them.'

Frank picked up the bat and threw it across the gap onto the deck of the police boat. 'You might want to use this then.'

Juan replied ' Yes, or I could put them back in the water and let the *Medusas* loosen their tongues.'

The engine of the police launch started up again and Juan shouted above the noise 'We must go now to catch the rest of the fish. We would be obliged if you take the cargo back to Mahón for us. My colleagues and the harbour master will meet you there.'

He waved to them as the cruiser pulled away. 'See you in the morning. You can sail that thing back home, yes.'

'No problem.' They waved back and watched it make its way toward the horizon to intercept the rendezvous boat.

Frank took the Yacht about and set a course back for Mahón Harbour.

Shivering in the cold night air and damp clothes, they found and wrapped themselves in some warm blankets and helped themselves to some of Sir Lionel's rare brandy. They were tired but relieved and took it in turns to steer.

They were just entering the harbour as the first rays of the morning sun painted the hillsides and houses with a golden glow.

They watched in silence, admiring the simple beauty of their surroundings. Frank put his arm around her.

Gulls wheeled overhead in the morning sky.

A gentle breeze kissed their faces.

A thought came to him.

Yes. Life in Menorca could be paradise.

But it could also be blue murder.

Printed in Great Britain
by Amazon

35223647R00081